Karen's Bully

Also in the Babysitters Little Sister series:

1 Karen's Witch

2 Karen's Roller Skates

3 Karen's Worst Day

4 Karen's Kittycat Club

5 Karen's School Picture

6 Karen's Little Sister

7 Karen's Birthday

8 Karen's Haircut

9 Karen's Sleepover

10 Karen's Grandmothers

11 Karen's Prize

12 Karen's Ghost

13 Karen's Surprise

14 Karen's New Year

15 Karen's in Love

16 Karen's Goldfish

17 Karen's Brothers

18 Karen's Home Run

19 Karen's Goodbye

20 Karen's Carnival

21 Karen's New Teacher

22 Karen's Little Witch

23 Karen's Doll

24 Karen's School Trip

25 Karen's Penpal

26 Karen's Ducklings

27 Karen's Big Joke

28 Karen's Tea Party

29 Karen's Cartwheel

30 Karen's Kittens

Look out for:

32 Karen's Pumpkin Patch

33 Karen's Secret

Karen's Bully

Ann M. Martin

Illustrations by Susan Tang

Scholastic Children's Books,
Commonwealth House, 1–19 New Oxford Street
London WC1A 1NU, UK
a division of Scholastic Ltd
London ~ New York ~ Toronto ~ Sydney ~ Auckland

First published in the US by Scholastic Inc., 1992
First published in the UK by Scholastic Ltd, 1997

Text copyright © Ann M. Martin, 1992
BABYSITTERS LITTLE SISTER is a trademark of Scholastic Inc.

ISBN 0 590 13967 3

All rights reserved
Typeset by Graphicraft Typesetters Ltd, Hong Kong
Printed by Cox and Wyman Ltd, Reading, Berks

10 8 6 4 2 1 3 5 7 9

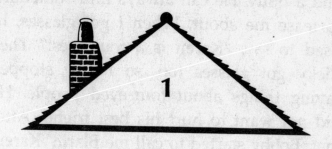

Blarin' Karen

I am Karen Brewer. I am seven years old. And guess what. I am married. My husband is Ricky Torres. He is seven, too, but he is a few months older than me. (Of course, we are just pretend married.) Ricky and I are in the same second-grade class at Stoneybrook Academy. Our teacher is Miss Colman. She is gigundoly nice. I just love Miss Colman.

Here is one bad thing about Ricky. His best friend is Bobby Gianelli. Bobby is a pest

1

and a bully. He can always find something to tease me about. When I got glasses, he used to say, "Karen is a four-eyes!" Then Ricky got glasses too, so Bobby stopped saying things about four-eyed people. He did not want to hurt his best friend. After that, Bobby started to call me Blarin' Karen. I guess I do have sort of a big mouth. But I do not think I blare.

Oh, well. Mostly I try to ignore Bobby the bully.

For instance, today in the playground I was busy with *my* best friends, who are Nancy Dawes and Hannie Papadakis. (They are in Miss Colman's class, too.) Nancy and Hannie and I were sitting on the ground inside the jungle gym. The jungle gym was a castle and we were three trapped princesses. We would not be able to escape unless triplet princes rode up to the castle on dragons and broke the evil spell that the Bad Witch of the World had cast upon us.

In order to alert the princes I had to lean out of the castle window and yell,

2

"Heeeeeelp! HEEEEEELP! Come and rescue the princesses!"

I did not expect anyone to answer me, but someone did. Bobby Gianelli yelled back, "Hey, Blarin' Karen! BE QUIET! I cannot concentrate on my marbles when you are making so much noise!" (The boys in my class have mostly only played marbles for the last ten or eleven days.)

I ignored Bobby. *Who will rescue us?* I shrieked.

Bobby left the game of marbles. He marched over to the jungle gym. He stood by it with his hands on his hips. "Be ... quiet ... Blarin' ... Karen," he said. Then he began to run around the jungle gym. "Blarin' Karen! Blarin' Karen! Blarin' Karen!" he sang.

Darn it. The princesses would *never* be rescued now.

I looked out of the window at Ricky, my husband. He was still shooting marbles. He was ignoring Bobby and me. It is hard for Ricky to be *my* husband and *Bobby's* best friend.

3

The bell rang then and break was over. So the princesses were never rescued and it was all Bobby's fault.

My classmates and I lined up and waited for Miss Colman to walk us back to our room. I stood with Hannie and Nancy. We stick together most of the time. We call ourselves the Three Musketeers. In front of us stood Bobby and Ricky and Hank Reubens. They were counting their marbles. Behind us stood Pamela Harding, who is my best enemy, and her friends Jannie Gilbert and Leslie Morris. They stick together all the time too, but they are too mean to be musketeers. Behind *them* stood the twins Terri and Tammy, and behind *them* stood Natalie Springer. Natalie always has droopy socks. When she talks, she lisps. Here is how she says her own name: Natalie Thpringer.

My classmates and I filed inside. While we were walking down the hall Bobby turned to look at me. "I lost half my marbles today, Karen," he said. "And it is all your fault."

4

Well, it was Bobby's fault that the princesses were not rescued.

I stuck out my tongue at Bobby. He does not scare me.

Bobby frowned. Then he said, "You think you are so great, Karen Brewer. Just because you have two families. But I think you are weird!"

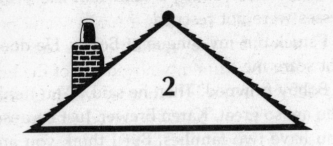

Good and Bad

Bobby Gianelli was right and wrong. I *do* have two families, but I am *not* weird. I think Bobby is jealous. I bet he wishes *he* had two families.

Why do I have two families? Because my parents are divorced. They got divorced a few years ago when I was just a little kid. See, I used to live in a big house here in Stoneybrook, Connecticut, with my mother and my father and my little brother Andrew. (Andrew is four now, going on five.) Then

6

Mummy and Daddy began to fight all the time. They said they loved Andrew and me very much, but they could not live together any more. So Mummy moved out of the big house and into a little house, which is also in Stoneybrook. (Daddy stayed in the big house. He grew up there.) Mummy took Andrew and me to the little house with her. The good part was that the fighting stopped. The bad part was that I missed the way our family used to be.

After a while, Mummy and Daddy got married again, but not to each other. Mummy married Seth. Seth is my stepfather. Daddy married Elizabeth. Elizabeth is my stepmother. Most of the time, Andrew and I live at the little house with Mummy and Seth. But every other weekend, and on some holidays, we live at Daddy's with our big-house family. And that is how we got our two families, one at each house.

Here is who lives at Mummy's: Mummy, Seth, Andrew, me, Rocky, Midgie and Emily Junior. Rocky and Midgie are Seth's cat and dog. Emily Junior is my rat.

Here is who lives at Daddy's: Daddy, Elizabeth, Andrew, me, Charlie, Sam, David Michael, Kristy, Emily Michelle, Nannie, Boo-Boo, Shannon, Goldfishie, and Crystal Light the Second. Charlie, Sam, David Michael and Kristy are Elizabeth's kids. (Elizabeth was married once before she married Daddy.) Charlie and Sam go to high school. David Michael is seven like me. (He sometimes calls me Professor, because of my glasses.) And Kristy is thirteen. I just adore Kristy. She is the best, best big sister ever. Plus she is a gigundoly wonderful babysitter. Emily Michelle is my adopted sister. She is two and a half. Daddy and Elizabeth adopted her from a faraway country called Vietnam. (I named my rat after her.) And Nannie is Elizabeth's mother. (That makes her my stepgrandmother.) All the others are pets. Boo-Boo is Daddy's cross old cat. Shannon is David Michael's puppy. Goldfishie and Crystal Light the Second are (what else?) goldfish. They belong to Andrew and me. (Andrew was the one who named Goldfishie.)

I made up special nicknames for my little brother and me. I call us Andrew Two-Two and Karen Two-Two. (I got the name from a book Miss Colman read to my class. It was called *Jacob Two-Two Meets the Hooded Fang*.) Andrew and I are two-twos because we have two of so many things. We have two houses and two families, two mummies and two daddies, two cats and two dogs. Plus, I have two bicycles, one at each house. Andrew has two tricycles, one at each house. We have books and clothes and toys at each house. (This is so we do not have to pack much when we go from one house to the other.) And I have my two best friends. Nancy lives next door to Mummy. Hannie lives across the street from Daddy and one house down. I even have twin stuffed cats. Goosie lives at the little house and Moosie lives at the big house. Of course, Andrew and I do not have two of *every*thing. For instance, I used to have only one Tickly, the special blanket I sleep with. I kept forgetting and leaving Tickly

9

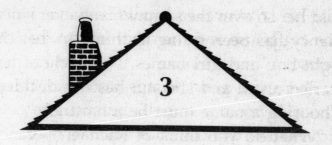

3

Bully Bobby

On most afternoons when school is over, Nancy and I ride home together. Then we play outdoors or at my little house or at her house. Sometimes we let Andrew play with us. Sometimes not.

Here is some exciting news. Nancy's mother is going to have a baby. Then Nancy will have a little brother or sister. So far, Nancy is an only child. But she is very glad she will be a big sister soon. Something else exciting is that Nancy gets to name the baby.

11

Honest. Her parents said she could. They told her so over the summer, and ever since, Nancy has been trying to think up just the right boy and girl names. Now school has started again and she still has not decided. Choosing a name must be a hard job.

"What do you think of Rachael?" Nancy asked me.

It was a Wednesday afternoon. Nancy and I were sitting on the front step at Mummy's house. Andrew was playing in the garden.

"Rachael is a nice name," I answered.

"And for a boy, how about Alexander?"

"That's nice, too." I paused. Then I said, "You know what I *really* think you should name the baby if it's a girl?"

"What?" asked Nancy.

"Karen." (Nancy giggled.) "No, really," I said.

"But I would get confused if my best friend and my sister were both named Karen. I know. How about something beautiful and fancy and old-fashioned. Like Patience Jane."

"Patience?" I squawked. "Patience is not

12

a name."

"It was in the olden days. So were Faith and Hope and Charity—"

Nancy was interrupted when someone yelled, "Yo!"

I looked up. I held my hand over my eyes to keep the sun out. Then I saw who was standing in my garden. I almost had a heart attack.

"Bobby Gianelli!" I cried. "What are you doing here?"

"It's a free country," he replied. (That is something my brother Sam says a lot.) "I can be here if I want."

I jumped to my feet. "No, you cannot! This is private property!"

Bobby stuck out his tongue. But he stepped back to the pavement. And Andrew ran to Nancy and me. He looked scared.

"Who is that?" whispered Andrew. (He tried to hide behind us.)

"That is Bully Bobby Gianelli," I told him. Then I yelled again, "What are you *do*ing here, Bobby?"

Bobby smiled. "I am moving to your street. I mean, my family is. We are going to be your neighbours soon ... So you'd better watch out."

"Why do we have to watch out?" Andrew asked me. He was whispering again.

"Oh, do not pay any attention to Bobby," I told my brother.

But just then Bobby said, "Hey, Andrew! I remember when you visited Karen at our school. I know who you are. Just wait until I move here."

I frowned. Then I thought of something. "I bet you are not *really* moving to this street, Bobby!" I yelled. "You are just saying that."

"Wrong!" replied Bobby. "We are moving into *that* house." He pointed down the street. He pointed to a house with a For Sale sign in the yard. Pasted over the sign was the word SOLD.

Uh-oh.

"See you soon, you dweebs!" cried Bobby. He ran towards the house.

Andrew crept out from behind Nancy.

15

Then he sat on the steps with us.

"Bullfrogs," said Nancy.

"Yeah, not fair," I added. "We have to see Bobby every day in school. Soon we will have to see him after school, too."

"Bully Bobby is scary," said Andrew.

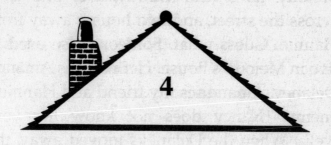

4

The 3 Musketeers + 1

That weekend was a big-house weekend. On Friday, just before dinner time, Mummy drove Andrew and me to Daddy's. So when I woke up on Saturday morning, I was in my bedroom in my old house.

I peeked out of the window. The sky was blue. The air felt warm. It was going to be a perfect September day. I decided to invite all my friends over.

Later that morning Hannie, Nancy and I were in my playroom with Melody Korman.

17

Melody lives near Daddy, too. She lives across the street, and two houses away from Hannie. Guess what. Someone else used to live in Melody's house. Her name is Amanda Delaney. Amanda is my friend and Hannie's enemy. (Nancy does not know her very well.) When the Delaneys moved away, the Kormans moved in. Melody is gigundoly nice. But she does not go to Stoneybrook Academy. She goes to a different school. So I do not see her very often.

Anyway, Hannie and Nancy and Melody and I had got dressed up. We had put on long slips and big high-heeled shoes and aprons and gloves and floppy hats. We were Lovely Ladies.

"Let's play outside," I said. "The Lovely Ladies should go for a stroll."

"Charming," replied Hannie.

And Nancy said, "We need parasols. We must protect our skin from the sun."

"Hmm," I said thoughtfully. "I do not think we have any parasols. We will have to use umbrellas instead. We can pretend."

18

We had just found four umbrellas and were tiptoeing around my garden, when Kristy called, "Karen! Telephone for you!"

"For me?" I replied. Who could be calling? All my friends were with me in the yard . . . Oh, maybe Ricky, my husband, was calling.

I ran into the kitchen. Kristy handed me the phone. "Hello?" I said.

"Hi, Karen! It's me, Amanda."

"Amanda!" I shrieked. "Hi! Kristy, it's Amanda Delaney!"

"I know," said my big sister. "But, shh. Remember to use your indoor voice."

"Sorry," I whispered. "Amanda, guess what."

"What?"

"A *bully* is going to move in right near the little house. His name is Bobby Gianelli, and he is in my class at school. Soon the only place I will be safe from Bobby is here at the big house."

"Boo," said Amanda.

"Yeah, boo . . . How come you are calling?"

20

"I miss you," Amanda replied.

"I miss you, too. When will we see each other?"

"I don't know. Mummy and Daddy have not said anything about driving to Stoneybrook. I hope we will come soon."

"Maybe you could come and stay here at Daddy's house."

"Maybe for a weekend, a whole weekend. I mean, if Hannie would not care," said Amanda. "Would we have to play with her?"

"Amanda, of course we would! Hannie is my friend. But listen, if you came to stay with me, you know what else we could do? We could go to your old house. A girl just your age lives there now. Her name is Melody. I have told you about Melody. We could visit her and then you could see your house."

"Excellent," said Amanda.

Amanda's mother needed to use the phone then so we had to hang up. I ran outside to tell my friends about the call.

"Awesome," said Nancy and Melody.
"Not," said Hannie. She was frowning.
Oh, well. *I* was excited.

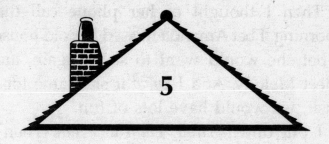

5

Amanda Delaney

I am reading a very excellent book. I have read it before and I will probably read it again. It is called *Sarah, Plain and Tall*. After supper that Saturday night I found my copy of the book. I sat down to read it. I sat in the living room where it is quiet. But I could not keep my mind on the story. I thought of Amanda instead.

I remembered the fun Amanda and I used to have when Amanda still lived across the street. Amanda was the person who started

23

the game of Lovely Ladies. It was her idea.

Then I thought of her phone call that morning. I bet Amanda missed her old house. I bet she would want to see it again, and meet Melody. And I *knew* if she came for a visit, we would have lots of fun.

I put down *Sarah, Plain and Tall*. Then I ran to the playroom. Daddy was there. He was playing Snakes and Ladders with David Michael, Andrew and Emily. (Boo-Boo was watching the game. His tail was twitching.)

"Daddy? Do you think maybe Amanda could come for a visit sometime? I miss her so, so much. And she misses me. We have waited very patiently for a visit."

"I think a visit could be arranged," said Daddy.

"Really? Could Amanda come here? To the big house? For a weekend?"

"An entire weekend?" repeated Daddy. "Well, I suppose so."

"Oh, thank you, thank you, thank you!"

"Yuck," said David Michael. "A weekend of girls."

24

I ignored him. (You have to ignore boys pretty much.) "Could she come in two weeks? For my next weekend at the big house?" I asked.

"I don't see why not," Daddy answered. "If it is okay with Elizabeth and Nannie. And if it is okay with Amanda's parents."

Elizabeth said the visit was okay! So did Nannie!

"Yeah!" I cried. I telephoned Amanda right away. "Guess what, guess what, guess what! Daddy said I can invite you for a visit! So do you want to come in two weeks? You can stay for the whole weekend!"

"Really?" exclaimed Amanda. "Sure!"

"Daddy says you have to ask your parents if it is all right."

"Oh, okay." I heard a *thunk* as Amanda dropped the phone. A few minutes later, she picked it up again. "Hi, I'm back. My mother and father both said I can visit. They will drive me to your house on Saturday morning and pick me up on Sunday afternoon. Also, they want to talk to your parents. They have to ask them some questions."

So the grown-ups talked for a while. When they were finished, I said, "'Bye, Amanda. I will see you in fourteen days!"

"'Bye, Karen! I can't wait."

On Sunday, I spread the good news to Nancy, Melody and Hannie. Hannie was the only one who did not think the news was good.

Nancy said, "Cool! I would like to see Amanda again."

Melody said, "Cool! I can't wait to meet the girl who lived in my room before I did. I hope she likes the way her room looks now."

But Hannie groaned. Then she said, "In two weeks? She will be here that soon? And she will be staying overnight? I wonder if I will be here then. Maybe my family will go away or something." Hannie checked. Her family was not going away. "Bullfrogs," she said.

26

"Oh, Hannie. It will not be so bad. You and Amanda used to play together sometimes. Remember?" I said.

"Yeah," said Hannie. "But I never liked her."

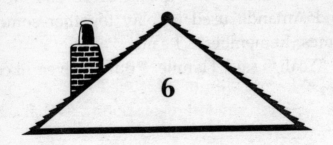

6

Bobby's House

On Monday morning I got some bad news. I got the news from Bully Bobby Gianelli in school. My friends and I were in our classroom. We were waiting for Miss Colman to arrive and start the day.

Hannie and Nancy and I were sitting on desks in the back of the room. We heard someone call, "Yo!"

"Yuck," I said. "Bobby is here."

"Yuck," said Hannie and Nancy.

Bobby wandered through the room. He

28

wandered right back to me. He stood in front of me and just stared.

"Take a picture. It will last longer," I said.

"So funny I forgot to laugh."

I stuck out my tongue at Bobby. "What do you want, anyway?" I asked him.

"I thought you might want to know something," he said. "I thought you might want to know that I am going to move into my new house in five days. So you'd better watch out, Karen. In five days I will be living on your street. Five days," he repeated.

"I can count," I replied.

It was Bobby's turn to stick his tongue out at me. Then he began to dance around the desks where my friends and I were sitting. "Oh, you'd better watch out, you'd better watch out!" he sang. He paused. "Hey, Karen, where will you be on Saturday?" he asked.

"What do you mean?"

"I mean, which family will you be living with? Your mum's or your dad's?"

Well, I was going to be at Mummy's. But

if Bobby did not know that, then I was not going to tell him.

Before I could answer, Bobby began to laugh. "You do not even know!" he cried. "You are so weird, Karen."

"I do know!" I shouted.

"She does know!" said Nancy.

"Yeah!" added Hannie.

I glanced over at Ricky. He was putting his books in his desk. He would not look back at me. Also, he would not look at Bobby. But when Bobby said, "Hey, Ricky, lend me your glasses," Ricky handed those glasses over.

Bobby put the glasses on. Then he said, in a high, silly voice, "Oh, hello, everybody. I am Karen Brewer. See my glasses?"

"Shut up, Bobby!" I yelled.

Bobby would not shut up. "Hmm. Today is Monday," he said. "Do I live at my mother's house or my father's house? I cannot remember... Where am I? Who am I?"

I looked at Ricky again. He had opened a book. (He was only pretending to read it,

30

since he was not wearing his glasses.) I could tell that Ricky was not going to help me. But at least he was not laughing at Bobby.

Luckily, Miss Colman arrived then. We all raced for our seats.

After school that day, Nancy and I took a walk. We walked down our street to the house with the For Sale sign in the garden.

"Soon this will be Bobby Gianelli's house," said Nancy sadly.

I nodded. "Yeah. What a shame."

Nancy was looking at the windows. "I wonder which room will be his bedroom," she said. "Maybe that one." She pointed to the first floor.

"I don't know," I answered. "There's the basement. Maybe that will be his room. Except it will be a dungeon. A dungeon for Bobby, the Evil Prince." I tried to laugh. But I was too worried about Saturday.

32

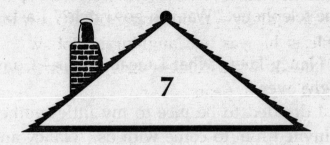

7

Moving Day

On Saturday morning I woke up in my room at Mummy's house. My stomach felt sort of funny. Right away, I remembered why.

It was Bobby Gianelli Day.

"Boo and bullfrogs," I mumbled. I rolled over and put the pillow on my head. I pulled the covers up as far as they would go.

Soon I had to get out of bed, though. My funny stomach had become a hungry stomach. I needed breakfast.

Andrew and I ate cereal in the kitchen.

33

When we were finished, I called Nancy on the telephone. "Want to go watch?" I asked her.

Nancy knew what I meant. "Sure! Come right over."

I decided to be nice to my little brother. I invited him to come with us. "Nancy and I are going to watch Bobby move into his new house," I said. "Do you want to watch, too?"

Andrew looked scared, but he said, "Okay."

"Do not worry. I will protect you." I put my arm around him.

Nancy and Andrew and I were not the only ones who had decided to watch the Gianellis move in. When we walked down the street, a whole crowd of kids was already there. Most of them were on their bicycles. Three of them were on roller skates. One was on her skateboard. They were crowded on the pavement. They were watching a removal van, which had just pulled into the driveway.

34

"Hey, look. The For Sale sign is gone," I whispered to Nancy.

"Why are you whispering?" she replied.

I shrugged. But Andrew said, "It is in case of Bobby. He might be hiding somewhere. He might be listening to us."

Bobby was not there, though. Only the removal men. They opened the side of the van. They began handing down boxes and lugging out furniture. Two of them were staggering through the front door with a couch, when a car honked in the street behind us.

Everybody turned around.

A man was parking a car. He opened the door and climbed out. So did a woman. So did a little girl. (She looked like she was about Andrew's age.) The last person out of the car was . . . Bobby.

"Yikes!" squeaked Andrew. "There he is!"

"Shhhh!" I hissed.

Bobby stood before us. He put his hands on his hips.

"Hi, Bobby," said Nancy nervously.

"Yeah, hi. Um, we came to watch you move in," I added.

"Why, how nice," said Mrs Gianelli. "You already have friends, Robert."

I nudged Nancy. "Robert!" I whispered, giggling.

Bobby glared at me. He waited until his mother and father and sister had walked across the lawn to the front door of their new house. Then he said to Andrew and Nancy and me, "What are you guys doing here anyway? Are you spying on me?"

"Get real, Bobby," I replied. "I mean, Robert. You are not *that* interesting."

"At least I know where I live," said Robert. "*I* only have *one* house. Not like some people I know."

Andrew stuck out his chin. "Being a two-two is not so bad," he said.

"Being a *what*?!" cried Bobby.

"A two-two. That is what Karen calls us. Andrew Two-Two and Karen Two-Two. So — so leave us alone, Bobby!"

Bobby stepped up to Andrew and leaned

36

over so that their noses were almost touching. "Hey, pip-squeak," said Bobby. "BOO!"

"Arghh!" screamed my brother, and he turned and ran home.

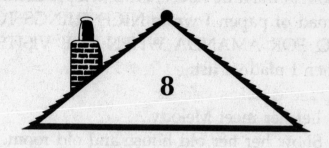

8

The 3 Musketeers + 2

I was so, so mad at Bobby. He was all I could think about.

"He called Andrew a pip-squeak," I complained to Kristy over the phone. "He scared him and made him run home. Plus, he—"

"Karen, give it a rest," said Kristy. "Forget about Bobby for a while. Think about Amanda's visit instead."

That was a good idea. I did need to think about Amanda's visit. I wanted to do something special for her. So one evening, in my

39

room at the little house, I found a pencil and a pad of paper. I wrote NICE THINGS TO DO FOR AMANDA WHEN SHE VISITS. Then I made a list:

1. Let her meet Melody.
2. Show her her old house and old room.
3. Be sure David Michael does not bother her.
4. Fix her an ice-cream cone.
5. Tell Hannie to put on her good manners.
6. Play Lovely ~~Laddies~~ Ladies.
7. Have a slumber party.

A slumber party! That was a great idea! We could have a *real* slumber party. Not just Amanda and me staying up late and talking — but guests and games and popcorn and Coke . . .

Now who should I invite (besides Amanda and myself)? Well, Nancy and Hannie, of course. The Three Musketeers have to be together at any party. And I should ask Melody. She and Amanda had lots in

40

common, after all. They were practically related. I decided five people was enough. That is, if Daddy would let me have a sleepover.

I ran to the kitchen and called the big house. I talked to Daddy and Elizabeth. "Puh-*lease* can I have a slumber party?" I asked. "I will only invite five people—including Amanda and me. And since Amanda and I will already be at the big house, I am really only inviting three people."

Daddy and Elizabeth said I could have the party. (In the background I could hear David Michael say, *"Five girls? Yuk!"*)

I did not care. I was too excited about my party. I thought about the things we could do. I decided we should: eat supper by ourselves in the playroom, watch a rented video, maybe try on Elizabeth's make-up, play Truth or Dare, bother David Michael, raid the refrigerator.

I hoped my friends would be able to come to the party. I hoped Hannie would want to come. I decided she would rather come than be left out.

41

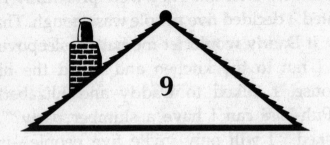

9

Saving Andrew

It was Tuesday. Bobby had been living on my street for exactly three days.

I was already sick of him.

Bobby had told everyone in Miss Colman's class that I call myself Karen Two-Two. He thought that was hysterical. Now he always called me Karen Two-Two. Only when he said it, he meant Karen Tutu. He would hold his arms in the air and pretend to be a dancing ballerina. In school, everyone laughed at him. And everyone called me Karen Tutu.

42

(Except for Hannie and Nancy. The Three Musketeers do not tease each other.)

Bobby was a pest and a bully, but I could stand up to him.

Andrew could not. He was three years younger than Bobby. And a lot smaller. He was extra afraid of Bobby.

On Tuesday afternoon I was in my bedroom. I was playing with my rat. I was making a wedding dress for her, in case she ever got married.

I was working on a rat-sized veil when I heard the front door slam downstairs. Then I heard Andrew crying. I ran to see what had happened.

I found Andrew looking for Mummy. Mummy had run next door to return something to Mrs Dawes. I would have to be the mummy.

"What's wrong, Andrew?" I asked.

"I cannot play outside any more," he said. He was sobbing.

"Why not?"

"I am too afraid. I'm afraid of Bobby. And,

um, other things."

"What other things?" I wanted to know. (I tried to think what Mummy would do if Andrew was upset. I was not sure. So I got him a dish of ice cream. Then I got one for me, too.)

"Thank you," said Andrew as we sat down at the kitchen table.

"You're welcome. What other things are you afraid of?"

"The killer bees," Andrew replied. "Bobby says they are coming to Stoneybrook. He says they are coming to our *street*. He says one little sting and, poof, you die. And he says you cannot even tell a killer bee from a regular bee. He says *any* bee could be a killer bee."

I frowned. I was pretty sure that was a big bunch of lies. "What else are you afraid of?" I asked my brother.

"Your glasses."

"My *glasses*? Why?"

"Because of the Martians. Bobby said the Martians send TV signals through your

44

glasses. He says that is how they spy on earthlings. Karen, could you please take off your glasses?"

"No!" I exclaimed. "I need them to see. I am not supposed to take them off, except when I am asleep. Or maybe when I take a bath. But that is all. You know that. Anyway, Bobby was telling lies. There are no killer bees here, and Martians cannot spy on us through my glasses."

"I don't know," said Andrew. And he began to cry again.

Ooh, I was so, so mad.

I waited until Mummy came home. Then I said to Andrew, "Do not worry. I will save you from Bobby."

I ran down our street to the Gianellis' house. Bobby was in the garden.

"Hi, Karen Tutu!" he called.

"Bobby Gianelli, you leave my brother alone!" I shouted at him.

"Who is going to make me?"

I paused. Then I said, "*I* am. I challenge you to a fight!"

46

Bobby stared at me. "I cannot fight a girl!" he replied.

"Are you afraid?"

"Of *you*? No way!"

"Okay. Then we will fight tomorrow after school," I said.

"Okay!"

"*Okay!*"

"OKAY!"

"Good." I turned around and walked home.

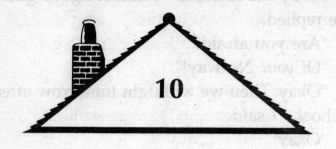

10

Taking Sides

"Hey, Karen! Are you really going to fight Bobby today?"

It was Wednesday. I was in the yard outside school. Natalie Springer had asked me the question. She was the fourth person who had asked me about the fight. And I had only been at school for five minutes.

"Yes," I answered tiredly. "I really am. This afternoon."

"Where?" Natalie wanted to know. "Maybe I will come and watch."

48

"They are going to fight in Bobby's front garden," spoke up Hannie. "Nancy and I are going to watch, too. We are going to get there early for a good view."

"*You're* coming?" I said to Hannie.

"Yup," she replied. "I am going home with you and Nancy today."

"Just to see the fight?"

"Just to see the fight."

"Wow." I felt kind of important as I walked into school with my friends.

I felt even more important when Pamela Harding met me at the door to our room. "Is it true?" she asked. "Are you going to fight Bobby?" (I nodded.) "It is about time someone did," said Pamela.

"Yeah," agreed Leslie Morris. "What a bully."

Across the room stood a group of boys. They began to laugh. They kept looking at me. Finally Hank Reubens said, "Karen, Bobby is going to destroy you! Why are you going to bother with a fight?"

"Yeah, you will only get hurt," added

another boy. He was not even in our class. He was just standing around, looking cool.

"Who are you?" I asked.

"I am in third grade," he answered proudly.

"How do *you* know about the fight?"

"*Every*one knows. And we are all going to come and watch."

I frowned. "Ricky?"

He was standing with the boys. He had not said anything yet, but I had this horrible feeling he was going to come to the fight—and cheer for Bobby.

"I can't come," said Ricky. "Um, I have a dentist appointment!"

I did not think that was true. I almost said, "But Ricky, I am your wife!" Then I decided Ricky might not like that. Instead I said, "You do not have a dentist appointment!"

"Well, I might."

Darn old Ricky. He was not going to cheer for Bobby *or* for me.

I looked around the classroom. I realized that everyone in it was staring at me. "Are

50

all these people really coming to the fight?" I whispered to Nancy.

"I think so," she replied. "Everyone is taking sides. The girls are going to cheer for you. The boys are going to cheer for Bobby."

"Except for darn old Ricky," I added. "He is too chicken to come."

"*You* are the chicken, Karen!" cried Bobby from the boys' side of the room. "*You* will not show up! Bawk, bawk, bawk . . . chicken!"

"Karen *will* show up!" said Jannie Gilbert. "And she will beat you!"

"With what?" asked Bobby. "She does not have any muscles. But I do. Look at this!" Bobby rolled up his sleeve. He bent his arm. He made his muscles bulge. "I have been working out," he informed us.

"Me too!" I cried. (I have never worked out.)

"Then show us your muscles!" called the third-grader.

"I will," I replied. "This afternoon at the fight."

51

Oh, no. I was in big, huge, gigundo trouble. I knew I could not beat Bobby. But I had to go to the fight. I did not want to be a bawk-bawk-bawk-chicken. So I turned to Ricky and called *him* a bawk-bawk-bawk-chicken.

Ricky just shrugged.

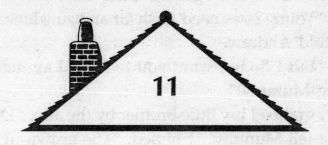

11

The Fight

*T*humpety-thumpety-thump. My heart was crashing around in my chest. I was standing in the front garden at the little house. I was looking down the street at Bobby's garden. It was crowded with kids.

Andrew was standing next to me, looking too. "Yipes," he said.

"I know . . ."

"Karen, you do not have to fight Bobby."

"Yes, I do. He scared you."

"That's okay. I will just stay indoors. Bobby

53

won't be able to get me then."

"Young boys need fresh air and sunshine," I told Andrew.

"But I do not want you to fight. I am telling Mummy!"

I grabbed my little brother by the arm. "Do *not* tell Mummy!" I hissed. "The grown-ups do not know about the fight. Now it is time for me to go down there. Are you coming with me?"

"Will Nancy protect me from Bobby?"

"Yes. You can watch with her and Hannie."

"Okay."

I squared my shoulders. I puffed out my chest. Then I marched down the street to Bobby Gianelli's garden. Andrew followed me. He tried to hide behind me so Bobby would not see him.

"After the fight," I said to Andrew, "you will not have to live like this any more. You will be able to go out in public again."

I saw Nancy and Hannie with a big crowd of kids from our class. (But no Ricky.) I took Andrew to Nancy. "Can you please watch

Andrew?" I asked her. "He needs protection from Bobby. But only until Bobby loses the fight."

"Where is Bobby, anyway?" asked Hannie.

"Isn't he here?" I said. I looked around the garden. I did not see him.

"Nope," Hannie replied. "We are waiting for him."

Maybe Bobby was not going to show up! That would be great. Maybe Bobby was just a big old bawk-bawk-bawk-chicken. I could say to everybody, "Bobby was so scared he did not even come to our fight." That would be as good as winning the fight—plus, I would not have to punch anyone. (And no one would have to punch me.)

"Yo, Karen!"

"Yipes! It's Bobby!" cried Andrew.

"Hide behind Nancy," I told my brother. "I will take care of this."

"Yo, Bobby!" I shouted back.

Bobby was stomping across the garden. He was trying to look mean. He showed off his muscles again.

"You don't scare *me*!" I said.

Bobby and I faced each other.

"Fight, fight!" chanted the boys. They had gathered on one side of the garden.

The girls (and Andrew) had gathered on the other. "Go, Karen!" they cried.

"Okay, Karen. You are going to get it!" said Bobby. He raised his fists.

I raised my fists.

And two hands clamped down, one on my head, one on Bobby's. I looked up in surprise. I dropped my fists.

"What is going on here?" asked a grown-up.

It was Mrs Gianelli. I guess she had seen us from a window.

Bobby and I glared at each other. "Nothing," I answered.

"Yeah, nothing," said Bobby.

The kids in the garden started to leave. Nobody said anything about a fight. "We were just playing," I added.

Mrs Gianelli looked like she might not believe us. But all she did was frown and let

56

go of our heads. Then she told Bobby to go indoors.

I ran home. I had not won the fight. But at least I had not lost it.

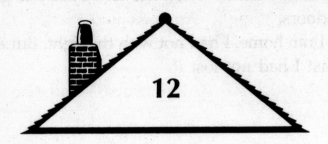

Chocolate Brownies

"Amanda's coming!" I sang. "Amanda's coming! Amanda-panda-sanda-tanda-danda-fanda-banda—"

"Enough, Karen," said Daddy quietly. "I know you are excited, but the rest of us are trying to talk. You are making it difficult to hear."

"*When* is Amanda coming?" asked David Michael for about the ninetieth time.

"Tomorrow-borrow-sorrow—" Then I paused. I lowered my voice. "Tomorrow in

58

time for lunch," I answered. "By this time tomorrow night, Amanda and Nancy and Hannie and Melody and I will be starting our sleepover."

"Goody, goody, gumdrops," said David Michael.

I eyed him. "David Michael, you are not going to ruin my party, are you?" I asked.

"He most certainly is not," Elizabeth answered for him. "Now please eat your dinner, Karen. You too, David Michael."

"Okay." I did go back to my dinner. But I was thinking about my party.

I wanted it to be perfect.

On Saturday morning, I got up early. I ran to the kitchen. I began to check through the cupboards. We might need to go to the shops.

"What are you looking for, honey?" Nannie asked me.

"Stuff for chocolate brownies," I answered. "We are going to make them tonight at the party. Let me see. Here are nuts and here is flour. Nannie, we do not have any cocoa powder!" I cried.

"Indoor voice," Nannie reminded me. "Karen, calm down. I will go to the shop today. I will buy cocoa powder. Please don't worry."

"Okay," I answered. But I did worry a little bit. First I worried about food. Then I worried about Hannie. I knew she did not really want to come to the party. She was just being polite. I thought of a slumber party I once had when *Nancy* would not come because we were fighting. Now maybe Hannie would change her mind and stay at home. I decided to call her.

"Are you still coming?" I asked.

"Yes," Hannie replied. She did not sound like someone who was looking forward to a slumber party. She sounded cross.

But I said, "Good. See you tonight." Then I called Melody. "When should I bring Amanda over?" I asked.

"After lunch." (I could tell Melody was excited.) "And guess what. I cleaned my room for Amanda! I hope she likes it."

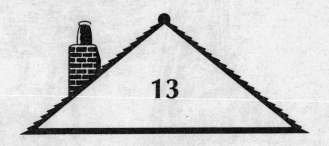

13

"Where Is My Fish?"

"She's here! She's here, Karen!" called Andrew.

"Yes!" I cried. "All *right!*"

I ran downstairs so fast I almost tripped.

"Slow down, Karen," said Daddy.

But I could not slow down. Amanda had arrived. We had not seen each other for ever. Didn't Daddy understand how it is with old friends?

I raced outside. Amanda and her father

61

were getting out of their car. "Amanda!" I shouted. "Amanda!"

Amanda and I hugged. Then we took her things to my room while Daddy and Elizabeth and Mr Delaney talked.

Later, after Mr Delaney had left, Amanda and I ate lunch. We ate it in the back garden. We had a picnic, just the two of us.

"When can we see my house?" Amanda asked.

"As soon as we have finished our lunch," I told her.

Amanda ate fast. She gobbled up her apple. She gobbled up her sandwich. Then she drank her entire glass of milk without stopping.

"Okay, I have finished," she announced.

I hadn't finished, but I stood up anyway. "All right. Let's go."

Amanda and I stood at Melody's front door. We were waiting to be let in. "Something looks different," said Amanda. She was frowning. "Hey, I know! They painted the door. It used to be blue. Now it is yellow."

63

Melody opened the door then. "Hi," she said. She looked nervous.

"Hi!" I answered. "Melody, this is Amanda, who lived here first."

Melody smiled at Amanda.

Amanda said, "Why did you paint the door?"

Melody shrugged.

"Um, let's go inside," I said. "Amanda wants to see her old room."

"I cleaned it up," said Melody as we were climbing the stairs. "Just for you, Amanda. I hope you like it."

"Oh, I will like it. I just loved my room. I still like it better than—" Amanda stopped talking, right in the middle of her sentence. She leaned over the banister. She looked down to the front hallway. "Just a second," she said. "Where is my fish?"

"What?" replied Melody.

"Where is my fish? Where is the fountain?"

A fish fountain used to be in the hall when the Delaneys lived in the house. The fish

64

stood on its tail. Water spouted out of its mouth.

"We had to take the fountain out," said Melody. "It scared Skylar. She is my baby sister. I guess the fountain is at the dump."

"The *dump*!" exclaimed Amanda. "You took my fish to the *dump*?"

Uh-oh. I thought maybe it was time to go home then. But Amanda would not leave. She wanted to look at everything in the house and garden. As we walked around, she kept crying things like "You painted my room, too?" and "How come you put a different fence around the pool?" and "Where is the tennis court? What happened to it?"

We were in the back garden by then. "We took the tennis court out, too," said Melody. "Daddy is making a vegetable garden there." I could tell Melody felt awful. And she wanted Amanda to feel better. So she said, "I know. Let's play Lovely Ladies."

Amanda whirled around. "Karen!" she cried. "You taught her to play Lovely Ladies?"

"Well, yes," I replied. "I taught Nancy and Hannie, too. You know that."

Amanda shrugged. She looked at the ground. "Let's go back to your house, Karen," she said.

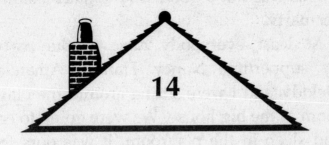

14

Lucky Duck

I was just an intsy bit worried about my slumber party. Not about little things like the food. Nannie had driven to the supermarket. She had bought the cocoa powder. But I hardly cared about chocolate brownies or supper or what movie we watched.

I was worried about my friends.

I knew Hannie did not like Amanda. I did not think Amanda liked Melody. And now Melody probably did not like Amanda, either.

67

This was not a good way to start a slumber party.

At least everybody *came* to the party. By suppertime Nancy, Hannie, Amanda, Melody, and I were sitting around the playroom at the big house. We were going to eat and sleep in the playroom. It was ours for the night. We could even close the door and be private.

Guess what we ate for dinner. Chinese take-away. It is my new favourite food. Daddy let me order it over the phone by myself. I ordered egg rolls, sweet and sour chicken, sesame noodles, and extra fortune cookies. When the food arrived we ate on the floor in the playroom. We put our plates in our laps.

Melody poked at a piece of chicken. "It is covered with orange stuff," she said. "*Bright* orange stuff. It is the colour of my raincoat."

"That *stuff* is sauce," said Amanda. But I noticed she did not eat any.

Hannie noticed the same thing. "Try the sauce, Amanda," she said sweetly.

Amanda gave Hannie a Look.

I felt like crying. "I guess Chinese take-away was not a very good idea," I said.

"Now see what you lot did?" spoke up Nancy. "You made Karen feel bad."

"We did not!" said Melody.

"You did!" I said.

"She started it!" Amanda pointed at Melody.

"*She* is named Melody!" cried Hannie. "Get some manners, Amanda."

"Why don't you? Anyway, at least I have good taste."

"What do you mean?" I asked.

"I mean that when *I* lived across the street, the fish fountain was running like it is supposed to. And the front door was blue. Nice normal blue. Who ever heard of a yellow door? That is stupid."

I thought Melody was going to yell, "It is not stupid!" But she did not. Instead she looked around the room at Nancy and Hannie and Amanda and me. A tear trickled down her cheek. Then another and another.

I glared at Amanda. "*Now* see what *you* did?"

Amanda hung her head. "I'm sorry," she mumbled. "It's just that . . . that she—I mean, Melody—gets to live in my house. I never wanted to move. I wish I were still living across the street. Moving is really hard. Melody is a lucky duck."

"Why?" replied Melody. "I had to move, too."

"Yeah, but now you live in my old house."

"But I wish I lived in *my* old house. That is why I asked Daddy to make a vegetable garden. To remind me of the garden at our old house."

"Oh," said Amanda. "Well . . . well . . . I think you will like your new house after a while. I always liked it." Amanda smiled then. She smiled at everybody. She smiled like she meant it.

"You know what?" I said. "I think we should skip dinner. I think we should just eat dessert instead. Who wants to make chocolate brownies?"

"I do!" shouted my friends.

We took the Chinese food downstairs and put it in the refrigerator. I knew Charlie would eat it later. He will eat anything.

Then I got out the nuts and eggs and flour. I was looking for the cocoa powder Nannie had bought, when the phone rang. "I'll get it!" I cried.

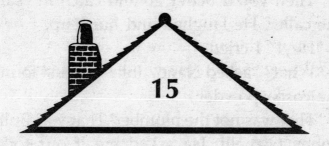

15

"Is Your Toilet Running?"

I grabbed the phone in the kitchen. "Hello?" I said. "Karen Brewer here."

A voice said, "Hello? Is your toilet running?"

The voice was deep, like a man's voice. Maybe it was the plumber. I decided to show Daddy and Elizabeth that I can be responsible when I answer the phone. (Sometimes they say I am not responsible.) So I put on my best grown-up voice. I said, "Yes, sir. Our toilet is running just fine."

73

"Then you'd better go and catch it!" said the caller. He laughed and hung up.

"Hey!" I cried.

"What?" asked Nancy. (She had just found the cocoa powder.)

"That was not the plumber! That was Bully Bobby Gianelli. He asked me if our toilet was running, and then he said to go and catch it."

"What a dope," said Hannie.

We forgot about Bobby. We made our brownies. (Kristy helped us put them in the oven. You have to be gigundoly careful around ovens.) We each ate two brownies. (Except for Kristy who only ate one.)

"Yum," I said. I was licking my fingers when the phone rang again. I dashed for it. Maybe a radio programme was calling to tell me I had won a million dollars. It could happen, you know.

"Hello? Karen Brewer here."

"Hello. I'd like to order two large pizzas with everything."

"This is not the pizza parlour," I said.

"And four Cokes," the caller went on. "And please deliver it."

"This is *not* the—Bobby? Bobby Gianelli? Is that you?"

Bobby laughed and hung up.

"Darn old Bobby!" I cried.

Bobby called us all night. Once Kristy answered the phone.

"Hello," said Bobby. "Are you interested in buying double-glazing?"

"No," said Kristy. "And I cannot talk to you right now. This is Mrs Brewer, Karen's stepmother. We are waiting for a very important call. From the phone company. The operator is going to tell us what to do about people who make hoax calls."

"Oh," said Bobby. He hung up. He did not call back.

But my family was already mad at me.

"Sherry was supposed to call me," said Charlie. (Sherry is Charlie's new girlfriend.) "She probably got an engaged tone all evening."

"I wanted to call the department store,"

75

said Sam. "Now I will have to wait until tomorrow. The store is closed."

"It is not my fault that Bobby is a bully and a pest!" I yelled.

"Indoor voice, Karen," Daddy reminded me.

I turned to my friends. "Come on, everyone. Let's go back to the playroom," I said. "Let's play Truth or Dare."

We returned to the playroom. But we did not play Truth or Dare. We talked about Bobby, the Pest of All the World.

"He is a pain," said Nancy.

"He scares Andrew," I added. "Andrew hardly ever plays outside now."

"Plus, Bobby got you in trouble tonight," said Amanda.

"I am glad he doesn't live on *my* street," said Nancy.

"You know what?" I said finally. "I am going to take care of Bobby once and for all. I declare war on Bobby Gianelli!"

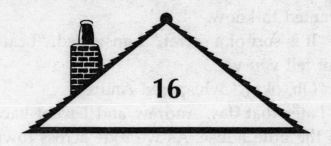

16

The Underwear War

On Sunday, everybody went home. Hannie and Melody ran across the street to their houses. Mr Dawes picked up Nancy. And Mrs Delaney pulled into our driveway to get Amanda.

"Goodbye, Karen!" called Amanda as she and her mother drove away. "I had fun. Thank you! Remember to tell me about... you know what."

"I will! 'Bye, Amanda! Thanks for coming!"

77

"What is 'you know what'?" Andrew wanted to know.

"It is sort of a secret," I answered. "I cannot tell you yet."

"Oh, okay," whispered Andrew.

Later that day, Andrew and I went back to the little house. As we rode across town I thought about my war. During dinner I thought about my war. After dinner I thought about my war. It was not going to be a war with guns or bombs, of course. But I needed a way to get back at Bobby.

Just before I fell asleep I had a great idea.

My idea was about washing. The Gianellis' washing. I had to wait until I saw it drying on the line at the back of their house. I finally saw it when Mrs Dawes was driving Nancy and me home from school one afternoon.

"Nancy? Did Bobby say what he was doing today?" I asked her.

"I think he is going to Ricky's house. Why?"

I shrugged. "Just wondering."

78

When we reached home I told Nancy I could not play with her. Then I went to Bobby's. But I did not walk down the street. No, I *sneaked* to the Gianellis' house. I tiptoed there through back gardens. I hid behind trees. I ducked behind bushes. I do not think anyone saw me.

At the edge of Bobby's garden, I crouched behind a pile of wood. I looked at the washing drying on the line. I saw socks and jeans and shirts and underwear. The underwear was what interested me. I could pick out Bobby's underwear easily. It was not the big underwear. That was his parents'. It was not the little frilly knickers. Those belonged to his sister. The medium-sized underwear was Bobby's. I darted from behind the woodpile. I ran to the line. I snatched one pair of Bobby's underpants. Then I raced home.

I hoped I was not stealing. I did not *think* I was stealing. I planned to return the underwear to Bobby the next day.

When I went to school in the morning I wore my backpack. Here is what was in the

backpack: my lunch, a reading worksheet, a jumper, Bobby's underwear.

I walked into Miss Colman's room. I pulled out the underwear. I waved it around. I held it above my head.

"Look, everybody!" I shouted. "Look what I have!"

"What?" asked someone.

"Bob-by's un-der-wear!" I sang.

Bobby leaped out of his chair. "Hey, that *is* mine!" he cried. "Where did you get it? Give it back, Karen! Give it back, Karen Tutu!"

I did not give it back. All the girls crowded around me. "I see Bobby's underwear!" shrieked Pamela.

"GIVE IT!" shouted Bobby. (He did not seem like such a bully just then.)

"Hey, nice pants, Bobby!" said Hank Reubens.

"SHUT UP!"

"Ahem," said Miss Colman as she entered the room.

Quick as a wink, everyone ran for their

81

seats. Bobby grabbed his underwear from me. He stuffed it in his desk.

"You'd better watch out, Karen Tutu," he warned me.

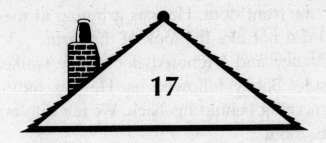

17

Minnie Mouse

Bobby was so, so embarrassed. Hannie and Nancy and I could not stop talking about him. Nancy and I were *still* talking about him on our way to school the next morning. (We talked softly so Seth would not hear us.)

"Bobby's face went red!" said Nancy.

"It was red almost all day."

"Bobby is gigundoly stupid."

"Totally."

When Seth dropped us off at school, we

83

ran through the gate. Bobby was standing by the front door. He was grinning at me.

I did not like the look of that grin.

Nancy and I ignored Bobby. We walked inside. Bobby followed us. He was hiding something behind his back. We ran into our classroom.

And everybody began to laugh.

I nudged Nancy. "Why are they laughing?"

Before she could answer, I heard a yelp from the back of the room. Hannie squealed, "Karen! Look!"

I turned around. Bobby was parading between the desks. He was waving a flag. No, not a flag. He was holding a stick. Tied to one end was a pair of . . . my knickers. And not just any knickers, my pink ruffled Minnie Mouse knickers. My *Baby* Minnie Mouse knickers. It is the most embarrassing underwear I own. I wear it because Nannie gave it to me, and I love Nannie.

"Robert Gianelli! Where did you get that?" I yelled.

84

"Same place you got my underwear. Off the clothesline. I mean, off *your* clothesline, not ours."

"You have *Baby* Minnie knickers?" said Pamela.

"Traitor," I muttered.

The boys were giggling hysterically. I could not believe they were seeing my underwear. I especially could not believe they were seeing my pink Baby Minnie knickers with the ruffles.

The whole class was laughing, except for Hannie and Nancy. The Musketeers would not laugh. They are true and loyal friends.

Hannie poked me. "Don't worry, Karen," she said. "I know how to get Bobby to stop flying your underwear." She raised her voice. "Here comes Miss Colman!"

Everyone ran for their desks. Bobby pulled my underwear off the stick. I snatched it from him. I shoved it in my backpack.

"Fooled you, Bobby!" exclaimed Hannie. "Miss Colman is not really coming yet."

But Bobby was still grinning. He had got me, and he knew it.

A few minutes later Miss Colman really did come into our room.

"Good morning, girls and boys," she said. "Please settle down."

I flumped into my chair. Next to me, Ricky was sitting quietly. As usual, he would not look at me. He just would not take sides. I let out a sigh. I wanted to tell Miss Colman what Bobby had done. I wanted to tell her how mean he had been. I wanted to say, "Miss Colman, Bobby embarrassed me. He waved my underwear around the room, so everyone could see it."

But I could not say that. If I did, Miss Colman would say, "Bobby, why did you do that?" And Bobby would answer, "Because Karen did the same thing to me yesterday." I did not want to get into trouble.

At break, Pamela started calling me Minnie. By lunchtime, my whole class was calling me Minnie (except for Nancy and Hannie and Ricky).

86

Boo. Boo on everyone. When school ended and Mummy had driven me home, I went straight to my room. I decided maybe I would never come out.

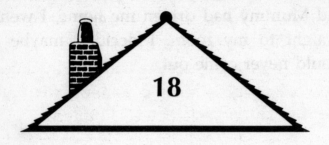

18

Andrew

Andrew changed my mind.

I had been in my room for one hour and six minutes. I had already made up two rules about never leaving my room. 1. I would never leave my room *except* to go to the toilet. 2. One other time I could leave my room would be to go to the big house. Then I would stay in my big-house bedroom.

I was not yet sure what to do about school.

That was when Andrew interrupted me. He knocked on my door. "Karen?" he called. "Karen? Can I come in?"

"Okay," I answered. (I had not invented any rules about people coming *into* my room.) "The door is open," I added.

Andrew stepped inside. He closed the door carefully behind him. Then he sat in my armchair. "Why are you angry at me?" he asked.

"Angry?" I repeated. "At you?"

Andrew nodded. "You were cross in the car when Mummy and I picked you up at school. You called me a twerp. And then you didn't eat a snack with me. We always have a snack when you come home from school. Also, you slammed your door. How come you're angry?"

"Oh, Andrew," I said. "You would not understand."

"How do you know?"

I shrugged. "Okay. I will tell you. I *am* angry, Andrew. But not at you."

"You act angry at me," said my brother.

"I know. But I am angry at Bully Bobby."

"Then why don't you call *him* a twerp, and slam a door in *his* face?"

"I would if Bobby lived here," I replied.

"Did Bobby do something to you today?" asked Andrew.

"Bobby and I are at war."

"Really?" Andrew looked impressed.

"Yes. Remember the goof calls he made during my slumber party? Well, after that I decided to show him who is the best bully. So I declared war on Bobby. That was the you-know-what Amanda was talking about. That was my secret. Bobby and I had an underwear war."

"What is an underwear war?" Andrew wanted to know.

I told my brother about the clothes line and Bobby's underwear. Then I told him how Bobby had made a flag out of my Baby Minnie underwear.

"Uh-oh," said Andrew.

"You know what the worst part is?" I asked. "The worst part is that I do not

90

know what to do next. But I *have* to get back at Bobby. I cannot let him win the war. If I do, he will keep teasing me. He will keep teasing you, too, Andrew," I added.

"Karen? Are you having the Underwear War because of me?"

"Partly," I admitted. I did not want Andrew to think he was trouble or anything, but . . . "I have to stick up for you," I said.

Andrew narrowed his eyes. "I can stick up for myself," he announced.

"You can? Are you sure?"

"No," said Andrew. "But I'd better try."

Andrew stood up. He marched towards my door.

"Hey, where are you going?" I called.

"To my own room. I have to think."

That was when I changed my mind about never leaving my room. Andrew was going to do something and I had to know what it was. He could not go around doing things without me. He needed me to protect him.

91

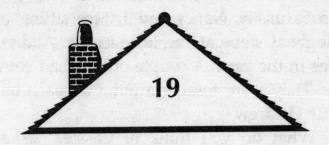

19

Snake Attack

Andrew was very quiet during the next few days. I knew he was still thinking. But Mummy did not. She kept saying, "What is the matter, Andrew? Do you feel all right?" She felt his forehead a lot.

I had different questions for Andrew. "What are you going to do?" I asked. "Are you going to do something to Bobby?"

Andrew would just shake his head. Or sometimes he would say, "I don't know." Then he would think some more.

93

* * *

On Saturday, Nancy and I were sitting on the front steps at the little house. Andrew was in the yard. A couple of kids had come by. They were tossing around a beach ball with Andrew.

"What do you think of Cassie?" asked Nancy.

"Who's Cassie?" I replied.

"No, I mean Cassie as a name for the baby. If it's a girl."

"Oh. Cassie is nice. I like—uh-oh."

"What's wrong?" said Nancy.

"Bobby is coming."

Nancy and I watched Bobby. He marched down the road. The little kids stopped playing. They watched Bobby, too. Bobby marched right on to our lawn and straight to Andrew. He did not look at Nancy and me.

"Hi, pip-squeak," said Bobby to Andrew.

"Hi," Andrew replied in a tiny voice. The other kids hung back.

"I guess you have seen the bees by now,"

said Bobby. "They are here, you know. They are in the neighbourhood."

"The killer bees?" asked Andrew.

Bobby folded his arms across his chest. "Yup."

A couple of Andrew's friends backed away. But Andrew said, "Well, I guess you have seen the snake by now."

Nancy and I glanced at each other. "What snake?" I whispered.

"What snake?" asked Bobby.

"The python," my brother answered. "The giant, escaped python. It is on the loose. It escaped from someone's house. It could be hiding anywhere. Pythons like basements, you know. And this python has huge, sharp teeth. You'd better get ready for a snake attack. You'd better be prepared."

"Pythons do not bite," said Bobby. "They squeeze."

"This one bites *and* squeezes," replied Andrew. And then, quick as a wink, he pulled a rubber snake out of his pocket. He flung it at Bobby.

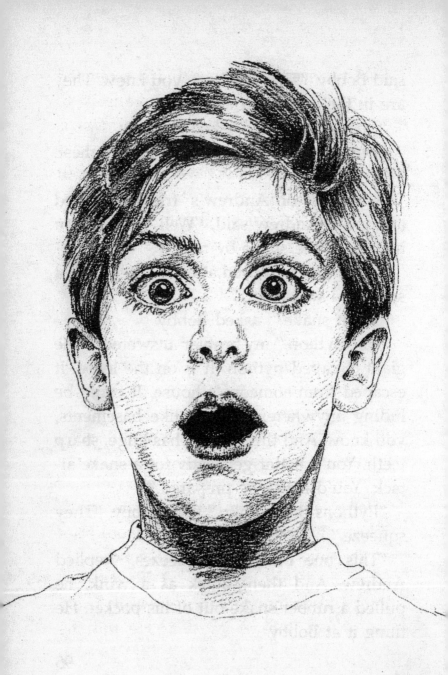

Bobby's eyes grew round. He screamed and jumped back. Then he turned angrily to me. "You see?" he cried. "You see? *This* is why I did not want to move. I liked my old house, where we did not have to worry about snake attacks. I never wanted to move. You guys are lucky, Karen. You and Andrew. You did not have to leave your old house for good. You get to go back and forth. I cannot go back to my old house." Bobby was almost crying.

While he was talking, I was remembering something. I was remembering Amanda and how she had not wanted to move. Melody, too. Amanda and Melody missed their old houses. I guessed that moving is not easy. I also guessed that Bobby teased me about my two houses because he really was jealous. Bobby wished he could live in his new house *and* his old house. That way, he would not have to leave his old house for good.

"Bobby—" I started to say. I stood up.

But Andrew interrupted me. "Wait. There is no snake, Bobby," he said. He put the

97.

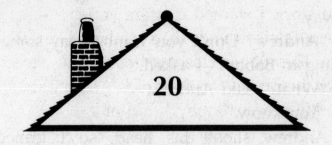

20

Andrew and Alicia

Nancy and I joined Andrew and Bobby and the other kids. I almost said, "Yeah, tell us about the killer bees," but I did not. I could tell that Bobby already felt horrible.

"Um," began Bobby, "there are no killer bees. I made that up, too. And—and I also made up the story about Karen's glasses. Martians do not really spy on us through them. You do not have to be afraid of Karen's glasses, Andrew."

99

"Okay," said my brother. He began to walk away.

"Andrew? Don't you want to say something to Bobby?" I asked.

"What?" said Andrew.

"You know."

Andrew shook his head, so I leaned over and whispered to him. Then Andrew made a face. But finally he said, "I'm sorry, Bobby."

Bobby kicked at a pebble. "Yeah. Okay. I'm sorry, too."

"I'm sorry, three," I added. "I am sorry about your underwear."

"Yeah," agreed Bobby. "I'm sorry about *your* underwear, Karen." (I thought Bobby was going to say, "I'm sorry it is so ugly and babyish." But he did not. I bet he wanted to, though.)

"Are you sorry about the goof calls?" I asked.

Nancy nudged me. "Karen!"

"Well, I want to know if he's sorry."

"Yeah. I am sorry about everything. Okay?"

"Okay."

Bobby went home then, but that afternoon he came back. Nancy and the other kids had gone home. Andrew and I were playing indoors.

When the doorbell rang, Andrew raced to answer it.

"Yikes!" I heard him cry. "Bobby is here!"

Andrew and I opened the front door. There was Bobby. Standing behind him was his little sister.

"Hi," said Bobby. "You guys, this is Alicia. She is four. Like you, Andrew. Do you and Alicia want to play?"

"We-ell," said Andrew. (Sometimes he does not like girls.)

"Alicia does not know any of the kids around here," Bobby went on. "I thought you might know some other four-year-olds. Alicia wants a friend."

"Maybe you could show her around," I said to Andrew.

"Maybe." Andrew inspected Alicia. Then he said, "How old are you *really*?"

"Four. I am really four. I just had my birthday."

Andrew grinned. "Oh! Well, I am almost five. So I am older than you. Okay, I will show you around. Come on with me."

Andrew stepped outside. He led Alicia down our front walk. Bobby and I looked at each other through the screen door.

"Well," said Bobby." "'Bye."

"Wait a second. I have an idea," I told him. "Come inside."

Bobby followed me into the kitchen. "What are you going to do?"

I picked up the phone. "Call Ricky," I replied. "Maybe he can come over. Then we could play together. All three of us."

So I phoned Ricky, and soon his father drove him to the little house. When Ricky got out of the car he saw Bobby and me. We

102

were waiting for him. Together. And we were not fighting.

Ricky grinned. He waved to us. "I'm here!" he called.

I shouted hello to my husband.

Then Ricky and Bobby and I played marbles. We played all afternoon.

Babysitters
— Little Sister —

Don't miss BLS 32

KAREN'S PUMPKIN PATCH

When lunch was over Daddy and I walked through the back garden. The vegetable garden is in a corner. (Luckily, it is *not* right next to the witch's back garden.)

"Okay. What do I have to do?" I asked.

"Before you do anything," Daddy replied, "I want you to see something."

He led me through the rows of aubergines and tomato plants and beans and carrots and turnips and potatoes. The vegetable garden was getting ready for autumn and winter.

I guess I had not been in the garden for a very long time, because I did not even know that in the spring Daddy had planted . . .

"Pumpkins!" I cried. "A whole pumpkin patch!"

YOUNG HIPPO SCHOOL

Something exciting is always happening at school in the
Young Hippo School series!

Off to School
Lisa, Ben and Max discover runaway buses, the Big Shirt
Race and a Santa who *takes* presents away!
Jean Chapman

Class Four's Wild Week
Mr Player can't keep up with his class – not because they're
naughty, but because they're too CLEVER!
Malcolm Yorke

Nightingale News
Read all about Jack, Chantelle, Melodie, Owen and
Mustapha's hidden talents!
Odette Elliott

The Grott Street Gang
Something HUGE, hairy and *banana-eating* is about to help
The Grott Street Gang with a dastardly dangerous deed!
Terry Deary

YOUNG HIPPO FUNNY

Have a giggle with a Young Hippo Funny!

Bod's Mum's Knickers
Bod's Mum has some ENORMOUS
and very useful knickers!
Peter Beere

Metal Muncher
Life's not easy when your baby brother likes to ... *eat metal* !
Kathy Henderson

Count Draco Down Under
Stacey has a strange new visitor – he's a VAMPIRE!
Ann Jungman

Emily H and the Enormous Tarantula
Emily H and the Stranger in the Castle
Emily H Turns Detective
Three funny books about Emily H and her special pet –
Theo, the world's most enormous TARANTULA!
Kara May

Professor Blabbermouth on the Moon
Tonight's the night for Operation Moon Cheese!
Nigel Watts

The Pirate Band
Captain Tump and his Pirate Band sail the high seas
in search of new treasure...
Ann Ruffell